ELIZA'S
BEST
WEDNESDAY

The Newberry Family

ELIZA'S
BEST
WEDNESDAY

Written by
Catherine Lalonde
and Louise Burchell

Illustrated by
Carol Sargent

Kids Can Press Ltd.
Toronto

We gratefully acknowledge the support of our families and friends. We are indebted to the staff at Upper Canada Village who gave their time and advice.

C.L., L.B. & C.S.

Kids Can Press Ltd. acknowledges with appreciation the assistance of the Canada Council and the Ontario Arts Council in the production of this book.

Canadian Cataloguing in Publication Data

Lalonde, Catherine
    Eliza's Best Wednesday

ISBN 1-55074-006-7 (bound)
ISBN 1-55074-032-6 (pbk.)

I. Burchell, Louise.   II. Sargent, Carol.
III. Title.

PS8573.A56E55 1990   jC813'.54   C89-090563-0
PZ7.L35E1 1990

Edited by Charis Wahl
Book design by Michael Solomon
Typesetting by Alphabets
Printed and bound in Hong Kong by Wing King Tong Co. Ltd.

Kids Can Press Ltd.
585½ Bloor Street West
Toronto, ON
M6G 1K5

90   0   9   8   7   6   5   4   3   2   1

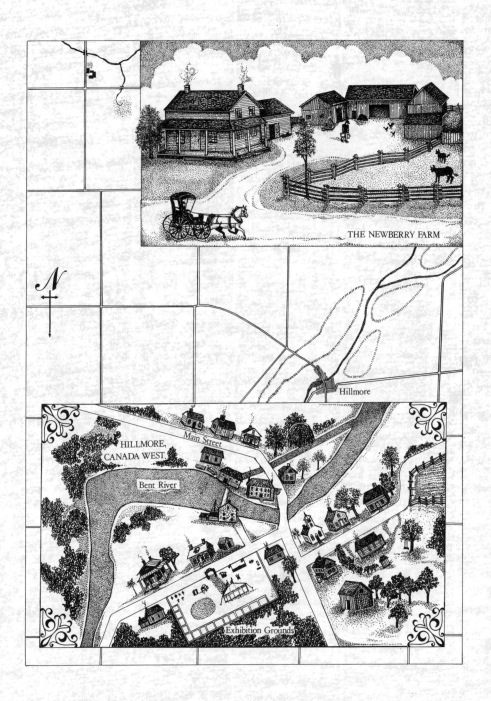

N

THE NEWBERRY FARM

Hillmore

HILLMORE,
CANADA WEST

Main Street

Bent River

Exhibition Grounds

ELIZA tumbled from her bed and hurried to the window — rain would be too disappointing. But the day was dawning crisp — perfect for the great Agricultural Exhibition!

Four whole weeks ago the family had gathered around the kitchen table while Father read the announcement in *The Gazette:* "The Agricultural Exhibition is to be held in Hillmore on the third day of October, eighteen hundred and sixty."

Eliza had always stayed at home with Mamma and little Thomas while Papa and James went to the Exhibition. James always came home with the most amazing stories: huge crowds, grand shows of livestock, and strange characters selling all manner of things!

But this year it would be different.

A quiver of excitement went right to Eliza's fingertips as she recalled Father saying to Mother, "Mary, I do believe that since Thomas is now five years old, the whole family can go to the Exhibition this year."

Eliza wouldn't have minded staying at home except for Hannah McQuinn. Hannah lived with her mother and two brothers in a small clapboard house down the road. She was tall, skinny, rude — and mean. "And isn't Eliza Newberry a wee babe! Let her go to the Exhibition and she'd get lost for sure. Never be seen again. And wouldn't that be grand!"

Eliza had blurted out that, not only was she going to the Exhibition, but she was entering her butter in competition. Hannah roared with laughter, "Save yourself the bother, wee Eliza. They'll not let it in, let alone give it a prize."

Eliza just smiled. Her butter may not be fine enough to win, but the Newberrys had other entries that were splendid. If they placed well, Father might purchase a coal-oil lamp with some of the money they won.

Eliza had seen a beautiful coal-oil lamp at Mr. Patterson's store in Hillmore. It had a sleek marble base, brass column and delicate glass body. The chimney glass was so clear it sparkled. The night Mr. Patterson first lit a coal-oil lamp such a glow was seen from his window that all the neighbours rushed over. They thought the house was on fire.

From her window Eliza could see Father on his way to the barn to tend to the horses. James' whole body was hopping up and down with the pump handle as he wildly drew water. In no time he'd be milking the cows and feeding the chickens.

Eliza worked the tangles from her long black hair. Then she made two braids and tied the ends with blue ribbons.

"Since today is so special, I get to wear my very best dress and straw hat." Eliza smiled, taking her yellow wool dress from its peg on the wall. When she had finished getting all the buttons and folds in order she studied her reflection in the little looking-glass. She could almost hear Papa chuckle, "Black hair, blue eyes and a fine determined chin — just like your Mamma's."

Then she giggled. Her mind was dancing with excitement.

Eliza thumped her feather mattress and pillow, pulled the woollen sheets and blanket tight, and spread her nine-patch quilt neatly on top. A quick glance around her room and she was down the stairs to the kitchen.

Mother was stoking the fire that Father had kindled. Thomas and Fan, the fat yellow house cat, were curled up on the settee keeping each other warm.

"Good morning, Mamma. Good morning, Thomas. Isn't it going to be a grand day?"

"Good morning, Eliza," smiled Mother. "The pork and potatoes please. We must hurry."

Eliza tied on her apron and fetched the breakfast foods from the pantry. Mother sliced the pork and potatoes for the frying pans while Eliza cut thick slices of bread and cheese. Then Eliza filled a small bowl with rhubarb preserves and

another with fresh, sweet butter. Just looking at the butter made her arms ache. It had taken her hours to churn the twenty-five pounds to enter in the Exhibition. She had washed the butter over and over with cold water and had worked in the salt that Mother had carefully measured.

"Hannah McQuinn's been to the Exhibition every year. She said my butter won't even be good enough to enter. Do you think that's true, Mamma?"

"Eliza, you're a very silly girl to listen to Hannah's prattle. It's the best butter we've made this fall. I only hope the judge will be equally impressed with my weaving."

Mother was entering twelve yards of her best striped flannel, woven from their own sheep's wool.

"Your flannel is sure to win the first place. The dollar and fifty-cent premium will be enough to buy a coal-oil lamp! James said a lamp costs sixty cents and oil costs a dollar a gallon. Maybe we can buy half a gallon, and then we'll have fifty cents left over."

"Forty cents," laughed Mother. "Patience, Eliza. Our

entries may not win a penny. Besides, Father decides how money is spent, and we don't need a coal-oil lamp. It would be nice, though, not to have to make so many candles."

Eliza hated making candles — dozens of them each fall. It was hot, smelly work!

Thomas chipped in, "I'm going to take Fan to the Exhibition. She's sure to win enough to buy a lamp."

"You can't take Fan," laughed Eliza. "Only the best crops and livestock from farms in the township will be shown at the Exhibition. House cats aren't livestock, Thomas."

"Eliza, stop chattering and put the food on the table," scolded Mother.

Just as Eliza put down the last platter of crackling brown pork and potatoes, Father and James came in.

James announced, "The chores are done and our entries are all loaded in the democrat."

Just to be certain, Eliza asked, "You didn't forget my butter, did you, James?"

"I brought it up from the root cellar myself," Father reassured her. "We loaded the apples, the cabbages and Thomas' carrots." Thomas had helped pick the carrots that Father had chosen to enter.

"Even the coop is in the wagon," added James.

James had chosen the poultry — the black-and-white speckled rooster, a black hen, and three red ones. Father was satisfied that James had selected their best birds.

The family took their places around the table. Father said grace and then helped himself to a heaping plate of pork and potatoes. Eliza felt full of butterflies. She had no room for breakfast.

"It will be a long time until dinner," insisted Mother, as she filled Eliza's plate.

When Father finished his second cup of tea he said, "I reckon my team has never looked better. If they perform well today, I'll be rewarded for the three years I've been working them together."

Champ and Monarch were pure black and strongly built. Father had raised them from colts. When they were two years old he had started working them as a team.

Papa smiled. "They're the best workers in the family."

Champ and Monarch could work all day in the fields, haul a heavy load or trot smartly to town.

"The boys at school say you're a fine horseman," said James. "And I didn't even tell them so."

Papa pushed his chair back from the table. "Our whole family has worked hard to prepare our entries for the Exhibition. I reckon James and Eliza have earned themselves a penny for today."

Eliza was so surprised she could barely add her "Thank you, Papa" to James', before Father and James went upstairs to change.

Never before had Eliza had two halfpennies at once! She held the large copper coins in her hand and thought of the wonderful things she might buy: a hair ribbon or a fine comb — or even candy. She decided it was best to give Mother her money for safekeeping.

While Eliza washed the breakfast dishes, Mother packed the large wicker hamper: roast chicken, plump bun loaves

and sweet apple turnovers wrapped in white cloths.

Soon, Father and James returned. Eliza watched with amusement as James repeated each step of Papa's final preparations at the wash-basin. They combed their wavy black hair, straightened their stiff white collars, and smoothed down the bows on their black cravats.

Thomas put on his jacket and cap and went with Father to hitch the team. James hefted the heavy dinner hamper and carried it out to the wagon.

Eliza was last out the kitchen door, just as the clock struck nine.

Father helped Mother with her roll of flannel up to the front seat of the democrat. Eliza settled in beside Thomas and James. Father hoped to cover the six miles to Hillmore by half past ten.

As the wagon jolted down the dirt road the boys chattered excitedly.

"We're sure to win more prizes than any other family in the township!" bragged James.

"Our things are the best there is!" echoed Thomas. "Papa said there are going to be hundreds of people there. Is that so, James?"

"Hundreds, Thomas. You'll have to stay with Mamma and Eliza so you don't get lost. I'm going to see the Exhibition with my chums." Then he lowered his voice. Eliza leaned closer as James continued. "Don't you two dare tell Mamma, but I'm going to see some of the attractions. Last year for a penny you could see a hundred-year-old goose. Joseph Ladd saw it. He said the goose had a long white beard — it was that old. You could just tell by looking that it was awfully wise."

James and Thomas talked and talked and talked. Eliza, lulled by the swaying of the democrat, the rustle of autumn leaves, and the warm morning sun, fell to daydreaming about the Exhibition — the grand displays and livestock shows. There might even be refreshments for sale: spicy gingercakes, gingerbeer or hard candies. She became lost in delicious thoughts until Mamma said, "William, I do believe that every vehicle on the road today seems to be heading for Hillmore." Indeed, so many families were going to the Exhibition this year that school had been closed for the day.

They were at the crossroads just half a mile from town. In every direction Eliza could see wagons, carriages and buggies loaded with barrels, crates, baskets and crocks.

Slowly, Champ and Monarch climbed the gentle grade of a hill. As they crested the slope, James shouted excitedly, "There's Hillmore! We've not far to go now."

Eliza, stretching to see better, exclaimed, "Look,

Thomas, there's the Exhibition grounds on the far side of town in Mr. Robertson's field."

The bright morning sun was lighting the great Exhibition Hall, the largest and most beautiful tent Eliza had ever seen. Two Union Jack flags proudly waved from the top. A large circle was roped off in the middle of the grounds. It was the show-ring, in which Champ and Monarch would be competing. The far boundaries were lined with stalls and pens to house the livestock.

Hillmore had never looked finer. Banners of every colour streamed from *The Gazette* printing office and Dunning's Tavern on main street. Gentlemen in silk top hats and ladies in fine dresses mingled with farm families in their Sunday best. Here and there, children in tattered clothes tagged behind their work-worn parents. Through the clatter of wagon wheels, the jingle of harness and the excited voices Eliza heard her name. There was the mocking face of Hannah McQuinn. She and her brothers were racing in and out among the wagons. "Did you bring your butter, Eliza?" The three guffawed and disappeared around a wagon loaded with barrels. Eliza hoped those McQuinns would keep running forever.

As the democrat neared Mr. Patterson's store Eliza held her breath. "Oh Papa, there's my lamp. Isn't it beautiful."

It also looked very expensive!

Across the bridge at the end of main street, they joined the line of vehicles waiting to enter the grounds.

The entrance was decorated with an evergreen arch, the motto, "Our Queen and Country," and a splendid crown studded with flowers and white snowberries. Beside the arch was the ticket booth, built especially for the day. It had a red, white and blue banner draped across it. At a bench inside sat sombre old Mr. Fowler. A white badge pinned to the lapel of his black frockcoat identified him as a member of the Agricultural Society.

"Good morning to you, John."

"How'd ya' do, William," growled old Mr. Fowler.

Eliza had to giggle. Mr. Fowler hadn't smiled for so many

years that his face had wrinkled in a permanent frown. A sharp look from Mother stopped Eliza's laughing, but the corners of her mouth crept back up each time Mr. Fowler spoke.

"I see you've paid your one-dollar member's fee," said Mr. Fowler, handing Father his white ribbon. "So you're in free. Mrs. Newberry has to pay, though, same as the general public. Children are free."

Father handed over the ten-cent admission fee for Mother. "A grand turn-out of people today, John."

"None too grand, some of 'em!" grumbled Mr. Fowler. He stabbed a gnarled finger towards a shabby wagon and booth behind the ticket office. "They're only here to wheedle money out of honest folk."

Folk like James! Eliza was shocked. So those are the attractions James is so keen to see.

Mother must have had the same concern. "James," she warned, "mind you stay away from those booths. They are sure to be run by quack doctors and artful swindlers."

BEWARE
OF
PICK
POCKETS!

"And mind the crowd," added Mr. Fowler, pointing at the startling handbills posted on the walls of the ticket office:

BEWARE OF PICKPOCKETS!

How glad Eliza was that she had given Mamma her two half-pennies!

"You have until eleven o'clock to get your entries tagged before judging begins."

Father bid Mr. Fowler good day and drove to the Exhibition Hall.

Near the tent there was a great flutter of excitement as exhibitors hurried in and out.

"James, stay with the horses until I return for the apples. Then take the democrat to the back of the grounds and unhitch the team — before you enter the poultry," instructed Father.

James got up onto the front seat looking proud as a peacock. Father lifted the large crock of butter from the democrat and lead the way through the crowd. Little Thomas followed, carrying his bunch of carrots. Mother managed a cabbage and her flannel. Eliza lugged the two large cabbages. "What a comical parade we make," she laughed to herself. Mr. Woods looked like an acrobat on a high wire balancing that bushel of potatoes, two heads of cauliflower and a cake of maple sugar. Mrs. Swatfiger's doing a juggling act — two jars of preserves in one hand and a quilt and hearth rug draped over her other arm.

Just inside the entrance Mr. Wilson, the Society's secretary, sat working at a long plank table. With a quill pen, he wrote a name and the entry on a cardboard tag. Another gentleman fixed the tag to the entry and took it away to be placed with others in the competition.

Hillmore
Agricultural Society

Class: Domestic Manufacturers: 12 yds. striped flannel.

Entered by: William Newberry

Eliza could hear a loud whisper. "There's old man Jones breaking the rules again. He's brought that same quilt three years in a row!"

"Would you look at that flannel of Mrs. Newberry's! It's not near as fine as mine," hissed Mrs. Reed.

"How dare she say such a thing about Mamma," thought Eliza. "Mrs. Reed is the worst old gossip in Hillmore — except for Hannah McQuinn."

Just thinking about Hannah made her nervous about her butter. The competition was going to be keen: she could see several crocks amongst the entries waiting to be tagged. That Hannah will tease her forever if she doesn't place.

When Father returned with the apples he placed each of the Newberry entries on the table. Mr. Wilson wrote Father's name on the entry tags. Some men had boasted to Mr. Wilson about their entries; others gave long-winded explanations of why their entries were not their usual high quality. Father did neither. His quiet confidence lifted Eliza's hopes.

Mr. Wilson announced, "Clear the hall. Clear the hall, please. It's eleven o'clock. The judges must begin."

"When can we see the results?"

"As soon as all the entries have been judged and arranged," replied Mr. Wilson a bit impatiently, as he herded the crowd from the tent.

Papa rushed off to see that James had entered the poultry and properly tethered the team. He wanted to look about the grounds, too. The family would meet in an hour for dinner.

"Can we see the animals first, Mamma?" begged Thomas.

Eliza was determined to forget about her butter and happily followed Mamma and Thomas towards the show-ring.

They joined the crowd gathering for the horse show. Colts, mares, stallions, and matched carriage teams would all take their turn in the ring before Father would show Champ and Monarch in the competition for general purpose teams. Eliza could hear men at the side of the show-ring making bets on which horses would win the day's premiums.

The judge, a stately white-haired gentleman, strode into the ring. He announced the first class of horses: one-year-old colts. The first colt, a light chestnut brown, baulked at the entrance. Its owner gave a gentle tug on its halter shank, but the skittish animal leapt into the ring with its feet dancing. The five colts that followed were just as undignified. Eliza liked the spirit of the chestnut colt and she picked it to be the winner.

The owners led their colts around the ring several times so the judge could see them perform. Then, they halted in a haphazard row down the centre of the show-ring. The judge examined each animal, stood back and pondered. Finally, he moved towards the light chestnut colt and stroked its mane. "I knew it!" thought Eliza with satisfaction. But just then, the judge turned and presented the first-place ticket to the owner of a black colt.

A tall skeleton of a man standing beside Eliza yelled, "That colt's got a bad leg. It's as crooked as tarnation."

A laughing voice answered, "Lost your bet, eh? Don't blame the judge 'cause you don't know a good horse when you see one."

The tall man shook a bony fist and pushed his way through the crowd. As he passed, his flapping coat slapped Eliza sharply on the face. The sour smell of chewing tobacco and stale cloth made her dizzy. Then a hand was on her shoulder and she was being pulled away from the noisy crowd.

"Eliza, mind you stay near me!" Mamma said bluntly. Trembling, Eliza clutched Mamma's hand as they headed towards the poultry show.

Chickens, ducks, geese and turkeys were clucking, squawking and honking nervously in their coops. James and his chum Joseph Ladd were like old mother hens themselves, cooing softly to calm James' flock.

Caught in the act, James greeted them sheepishly. "I was just telling Joe how I picked out our poultry, Mamma."

Eliza and Joe grinned at each other — James had told Joe the same story at school at least fifty times!

To change the subject James offered to show them two coops of fancy birds among the large show of common fowl.

"This black and white bird is a Silver Spangled Hamburg. Isn't it a beauty!" Before they had a chance to admire this fine bird, Thomas moved to the second coop.

"This bird ain't got any feet!" shouted Thomas, pointing to a buff-coloured bird strutting back and forth.

"Sure it does, Thomas. That's a Cochin China," explained James. "Its feet are under all 'em feathers on its legs."

Thomas stuck his nose right up to the edge of the coop and twisted around to see under the feathers. When the bird lifted its foot Thomas called, "It's got big fat feet. That's why they're all covered up with 'em feathers."

Now Thomas wanted to see the livestock. James was not impressed with the few pigs and quickly passed them by, but Eliza peeked through the boards of one pen and saw a pig that stood taller than Thomas.

Eliza counted nine pens filled with common sheep like those the Newberrys had at home. But the sheep in the next three pens were huge and their fleece seemed to trail on the ground.

"Mamma, what a lot of wool on those big sheep,"

exclaimed Eliza, thinking of all the yarn Mother could spin.

James sounded very grown up and wise. "There's many a supper on that fine animal. These Leicester are the most popular improved breed in the township. They've a good fleece and fine mutton, too."

Thomas raced ahead. "There are lots and lots of cows here just like ours," he called. They followed to admire the beefy, short-horned cattle. Roan, white and red Durham cows were tied along the fence.

James was more interested in the red and white Ayrshire bull penned behind a strong board fence. Long, upright horns gave the slender animal a majestic look.

"One day I'll have the finest livestock in the township. My cattle will all be Ayrshire." James looked around to gauge the effect of his announcement, but only Thomas looked impressed. "Papa thinks the Ayrshire a better milker," he went on. "I reckon we'll soon be having some on

our farm. We'd have lots more milk for Mamma to make into cheese."

"And lots more butter to churn!" thought Eliza. But she knew the family could make good use of the money that extra butter and cheese would bring.

Eliza, Thomas and Mother left James at the livestock and walked to the entrance of the Exhibition. To their left a neat row of implements stretched the width of the grounds. The genius of local carriage makers was proven by a fine display of buggies, democrats and sturdy, gaily painted wagons.

The Adams Foundry and Machine Works had a display of their products. Their salesman was about forty years of age. His clothes carried the acrid odour of molten metal, and his black, scarred hands gave proof to his words.

"I've worked for the Adams Foundry for ten years. Their reputation as the finest manufacturers of ploughs, harrows and woodstoves is known and respected throughout the district." Placing one hand solidly on a steel plough, he continued. "The judges in their wisdom have seen the merits of our improved steel plough and have awarded the grand prize of ten dollars to the Adams Foundry. I believe that this plough will soon be favoured by all progressive farmers. It can turn a furrow better than any other — evenly and cleanly."

At the edge of the crowd the ladies were admiring the iron cookstove, cast in a pattern of acorns and leaves. The salesman turned to them. He looked at Mother and said, "Not only is this cookstove pleasing to the eye, ma'am, but it has many advantages to the practical housewife like yourself. Notice the solidly built boxes of cast iron.

"Ladies, you can have four pots boiling on these four boiling holes, a roast cooking in one oven and bread baking in the other, all at the same time! Not only is this the most efficient stove on the market, but it's guaranteed to do more cooking with less wood."

As the women pressed closer to examine the cookstove Eliza and Thomas were squeezed to the back of the crowd. Suddenly, the ladies' chatter was drowned out by the jingle of harness bells and the rattle of tinware. A wagon, painted bright blue and yellow, clattered into the Exhibition grounds.

"It's the Yankee pedlar!" called several voices.

A young man sat on the driver's seat. He was dressed most fashionably, quite unlike any pedlar Eliza had ever seen. His trousers, waistcoat and baggy coat were all cut from a green-and-grey checkered cloth that made him look like an elf. His laughing smile and keen black eyes added to his impish looks.

The sides of the pedlar's wagon were higher than a man's head and lined with a wonderful array of wares on hooks and racks. Thomas, delighted by the clatter of tinware, counted out all he saw. "There's a milk pail and two big canisters and six little ones and three candlesconces — and water pails and tea kettles of every size."

The wicker baskets, wooden tubs, iron pots and kettles tied to the top of the wagon swayed precariously as the pedlar halted his team. Eager helpers from the crowd un-hitched the weary team and led them away. The pedlar jumped down from the wagon and called in a nasal twang, "Who'll buy? Who'll buy?"

Eliza and Thomas watched entranced. Like magic, one surprise after another appeared in his hands — a tin whistle, a shining jack-knife, a glittering necklace with paste baubles. "Like the jewels in the crown — fit for any lady," drawled the pedlar.

Then he opened the doors on the back of his wagon and pulled out rolls and rolls of cotton. Soon, ladies were handling the brightly coloured prints and calicos, dreaming of dresses, curtains, chemises and petticoats.

Next he pulled out two small trunks and unpacked their contents: steel pens and nibs, wooden matches, lead pencils, plain and fancy buttons, hair ribbons, small scissors, pins and needles.

Eliza thought, "Lavender scented soap. Oh dear, three pennies! A lead pencil — costs one-and-a-half pennies. The steel scissors and fancy hair combs are far too expensive. I

could buy a hair ribbon or a steel pen and nibs — or some fancy buttons for a new dress.''

Just when Eliza had decided that she would buy a hair ribbon the pedlar brought out five tin canisters and opened the lids. The scent of peppermint, lemon drop, horehound, raspberry and ginger filled the air. Eliza's mouth watered. What a decision! A red hair ribbon or candy! Eliza was almost relieved when Mother suggested she think about it and make her purchase later in the day.

The sun, high in the sky, reminded Mother that Father would be wanting his dinner. Reluctantly, Eliza followed Mother and Thomas. Near the ticket office they crossed the path that led to the great Exhibition Hall. With so much to see Eliza had given little thought to their entries. But now she wondered about her butter. She looked towards the hall, but all was quiet — not a soul moved in or out.

As they passed the ticket office, Eliza saw a noisy crowd gathered around the quack doctors and artful swindlers. A scruffy man stood on a wagon, his black hair dangled over his lank, grey cheeks. He held up a small brown bottle and bawled, "Cooper's Miracle Oil! Cures toothaches, sprains, fever, sore throats, burns, deafness, liver complaints and more. Throughout the country, people will attest to its miraculous curing powers. Why only a short distance from here is a man who is living proof of the powers of Cooper's Miracle Oil. For three long years he suffered pain that was unbearable to witness. Couldn't lift his head from the pillow without the help of his good woman. Nothin' stopped the pain or gave him strength until he tried Cooper's Miracle Oil. In just three days — three days — the pain was gone. Vanished. The third morning he got up from his bed and went out and chopped wood — strong and restored!"

An ancient, bent man shuffled forward to purchase the wonder cure. Others followed. The old scoundrel took their money and thanked them with a toothless grin.

Eliza chuckled, thinking that last year he was probably displaying the hundred-year-old goose.

"Eliza, follow closely, now." Mother was marching forward, eyes straight ahead, past the rowdy onlookers.

Over the next gawdy booth was an ornate sign:

PROFESSOR GRANT,

PHRENOLOGIST.

UNLOCK THE HUMAN MYSTERIES

THAT FORETELL YOUR FUTURE.

Eliza couldn't help staring. Professor Grant was very large, his face almost covered by an enormous red beard that flowed down his chest. Buttoned around his ample stomach was a waistcoat of rich gold, red and peacock-blue silk. His voice boomed over the crowd. Eliza's steps became shorter and slower.

"I unlock the mysteries of the mind by making a careful study of the head. Aided by these complex charts and drawings I can foretell your future."

The Professor stared at the crowd. "For a copper, in the total privacy of my booth, I will disclose to you what your future holds."

Motioning to a farmer, he said, "Sir, would you like me to examine the heads of your children?"

"Well," said the farmer, pausing, "I rather guess they don't need it. The old woman goes over 'em with a fine-tooth comb once a week."

Onlookers roared with delight, but Eliza almost choked on her laugh. James! What was he doing in the crowd? What if Mamma noticed? She rushed to catch up with Mother and Thomas, who were heading toward the maple grove at the back of the grounds.

Papa was waiting for them. He had removed the two seats from the democrat and placed them on the ground so

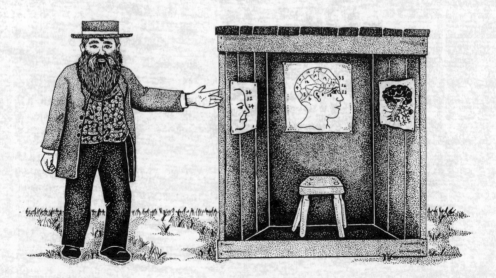

they could sit and eat their dinner. Mother quickly unpacked the hamper, spread a white cloth on the ground and arranged the plates, knives and forks. James and his friends came sauntering up the path just as Mother laid out the food. Eliza was starving! Mother's roast chicken and lemonade had never tasted better.

After dinner, Mother and Father lingered about the democrat visiting with their neighbours. James ran off to meet Joe in the maple grove, and Eliza followed. They soon found Joe with other boys and girls. Hannah, Albert and Henry McQuinn were there, too! Albert's raw red knees poked out of the holes in his trousers. Henry's face looked like it hadn't seen soap and water in a week. Eliza hung back, hoping Hannah wouldn't notice her. The boys' stories of their morning's adventures soon had everyone's attention. Eager to have his turn, James whispered to Eliza, "You won't tell, will you, Eliza?"

"Mamma said you were to stay clear of wicked attractions."

"If Mamma finds out, Eliza, you know I'll catch a walloping from Papa when we get home," pleaded James.

Eliza considered.

"Eliza Newberry! You'll never hear what the Professor told me if you don't promise to keep it a secret."

This was too much for Eliza's curiosity. She promised James she'd never, never tell.

James adjusted his cravat and turned his hat in his hands. Then, he stepped forward.

"I reckon Professor Grant is the smartest man that ever lived. Just by examining a person's head he can tell all about them. You see that's 'cause he understands the human brain. Why, he even had diagrams of the brain and every part has a name. Some of 'em names on that chart was this long."

James stretched his arms wide. A murmur of "ahs" went through the audience.

"He called the parts organs and the more you exercise 'em the bigger they get. If they're too small, you're bound to be one of those shiftless lads, and if they're too big you ain't going to be a gentleman, for sure. The Professor says it's all in knowing how to exercise the organ just right. Well, I guess I've been exercising my brain right 'cause the Professor examined my brain and — "

"O, aye, and how'd the Professor see inside yerself?" mocked Hannah. "It's not possible to do the like."

"Well, that's the most remarkable part. He just laid his hands like so," explained James, placing his hands over his head. "The Professor could feel the brain organs 'cause they're lumps on your head. The ones right under my fingers show I'm ambitious." Moving his hands to the back of his neck James continued. "This strong part of my brain shows I'll be good at farming. One day I'll own lots of land and be a gentleman farmer!"

Many of the boys tried examining their own heads to see if they were as ambitious as James. Eliza knew she would never have the courage to go to Professor Grant. What if some dark misfortune lay ahead? It was better not to know.

A sudden stir of activity around the wagons sent the children scurrying back to their parents. The judging was finished. The Exhibition Hall was open. Father decided it was time to prepare his team for the show-ring. Eliza

whispered, "Good luck, Papa," as he hurried away. James eagerly ran off to see the results of the poultry judging.

Mother, with Eliza and Thomas in hand, anxiously joined the great crowd jamming into the Exhibition Hall. In the very centre of the tent stood a towering display of flowers: fresh marigolds and asters, potted geraniums and ferns filled the top two tiers. Autumn bouquets encircled the bottom shelf. The display was topped with an intricate design of dried flowers and evergreen that spelled out "The Floral Temple."

Long tables were filled with entries: quilts, knitted mitts, stockings, bread, preserves, fruits, vegetables, harness, leather boots, crochet and embroidered work. Sacks of wheat, oats, peas, barley, rye and corn were crammed into every nook.

The jostling crowd was so large Eliza feared they would never find their entries. However, Mother confidently threaded a path through the confusion right to the table filled with home-manufactured yarns, cloth and blankets. There, in the middle, was Mother's flannel! Eliza searched for the first-place ticket.

"I can't find it!" wondered Eliza. "It must be — oh! Something's wrong! That's a second-place ticket."

Crushed, Eliza looked up at Mother.

"Miss Barcley's flannel placed first," Mother announced, smiling.

Before Eliza could object, a crisp voice from behind them said, "Your flannel is very fine, Mrs. Newberry."

"Thank you, Miss Barcley. I feel quite pleased that my flannel should place second to yours."

Spinster Barcley was the best weaver in the whole district. In fact, she had taken first place in the striped, plaid and white flannel classes. Eliza thought, "If it weren't for Miss Barcley, Mother would have won. But Mamma's flannel certainly deserves the premium for second place." One dollar and twenty-five cents.

While Mother and Miss Barcley chatted, Eliza looked about impatiently for her butter. In the show of dairy products she could see four wooden firkins standing on the floor, each containing eighty pounds of butter. She saw cheeses and butter crocks but she could not see hers. She stood on tiptoe and then wormed down to peer under arms. But it was no use!

Just when Eliza thought she would burst, Mother said good day to Miss Barcley. Squeezing through the crowd they came to the row of butter crocks. Grandly displayed at the front of the table was Eliza's crock of butter — with a bright

THIRD PRIZE

FIRST PRIZE

SECOND PRIZE

Hillmore
Agricultural Society
Class: Dairy Products:
Butter - 25 lbs.
Entered by: William Newberry

Gazette Printing Office

red ticket! Eliza just stared — she had never dared to hope she would place first!

All around men and women were congratulating Mother on their win. Eliza could feel her cheeks burning as Mother told them that it was Eliza who had churned and washed the butter.

"Just wait till I tell that Hannah McQuinn!" thought Eliza with satisfaction, and then felt just a bit ashamed.

Thomas nudged closer. "How much did we win?"

"One dollar and fifty cents," whispered Eliza.

Enough to buy a coal-oil lamp! Eliza wanted to make a wish, but Thomas tugged impatiently on her arm.

"Let's go find my carrots."

A table was filled with parsnips, turnips, beets, onions and other garden produce. Bushel baskets of potatoes, huge pumpkins, squash and watermelon covered the floor around the table.

Eliza quickly found Thomas' carrots and lifted him up for a better look. "You've won a blue ticket, just like Mamma's. That's a fifty-cent premium for second." Thomas clapped his hands in joy.

"Our three cabbages haven't placed," said Mother. "But, my, Mr. Jackson's prize-winners are very fine and compact."

"These are a new variety," Mr. Jackson explained. "Winningstats. Recommended by the Agricultural Society. They keep well in winter."

Mother thought she would try some in their garden next year.

The last table was filled with a large show of apples. Thomas was quick to find Father's half bushel of snows.

"Papa won a second! Why didn't he win first place, Eliza? How much does second pay?"

"Papa gets seventy-five cents. I don't understand why Papa's didn't get first, either," confessed Eliza.

Indeed, Father's snow apples looked identical to the basket that placed first.

"Well," insisted Thomas, "I like ours best."

Someone else found the Newberrys' apples tempting, too. From the midst of the crowd a hand darted out, seized an apple, and disappeared.

"Mamma!" cried Eliza. "Those boys are stealing our apples!"

Her outcry caused a flurry of excitement as everyone tried to find the culprit. Then people realized that other fruit and vegetables were being stolen, too. Young men and boys were jostling and elbowing, and helping themselves to whatever they fancied.

"The Society should do something to stop this," protested an exhibitor.

Doctor Scott shook his head sadly. "They'll just run you ragged. These big boys are too clever at their sport. You'll just be wasting your time trying to catch them."

"It's shameful," huffed spinster Barcley, "when the belongings of decent folks aren't safe from such pranksters. I intend to stay right here and watch my entries."

Mother became alarmed over the safety of her flannel.

"Miss Barcley, would you be so kind as to keep an eye on our entries, as well? William will soon be showing our team and we would like to see the show."

"With pleasure, Mrs. Newberry. The ruffians!"

Eliza felt sure no one would be foolish enough to risk being caught by stern spinster Barcley. With Mother's permission Eliza hurried off to find James at the poultry display.

The broad grin on his face told her that he had placed first. Eliza eagerly told James of the premiums the family had won on the flannel, butter, carrots and apples. He tallied their winnings. "With the dollar for first on my poultry — that makes five dollars!"

"Five dollars! That's a great deal of money," exclaimed Eliza wide-eyed. "Do you think Papa will buy the lamp?"

"I reckon if Champ and Monarch do well Papa will be so pleased, he'll be going to town next week for sure to — "

Hannah's voice broke in. "Well, you'll both be wishing ya had stayed to home with your poor, miserable entries."

Her mean face appeared over the coop. Henry and Albert grinned through the slats at Eliza.

"Bet you McQuinns haven't one of these." James boldly stuck his red ticket right in front of Hannah's nose. "Eliza has one just like it — she won first place on her butter!"

Hannah was so taken aback that she was tongue-tied. Suddenly, such a racket arose from the coop that Eliza and James jumped. The black hen was beating its wings frantically on the sides of the coop. The three red hens were squawking in one corner and the poor rooster was scratching

wildly on the floor boards.

"Albert and Henry are pulling the tail feathers from our rooster!" screamed Eliza.

James leaped towards the boys. "Get away you two — or I'll give you what ya deserve!" he roared. The McQuinns fled into the crowd.

"Those stupid boys would have tormented him to death," sputtered James, anxiously inspecting his bird.

"That was brave of you to send the McQuinns on their way," said Eliza quietly. "Hannah'll not be bothering us again soon."

Embarrassed by Eliza's praise, James scuffed his feet in the dirt. Abruptly, he asked, "Have you spent your money yet, Eliza?"

"Not yet. I saw a pretty hair ribbon at the pedlar's, but I've decided to buy some horehound candy. I'll share some with you." James grinned from ear to ear at the thought of a candy treat. Eliza added, "Just for being so brave."

James decided he'd better stay near Eliza to make sure she didn't buy that hair ribbon instead. "We'd best hurry. Papa will soon be showing Champ and Monarch."

They met up with Mother and Thomas, and James led the family through the crowd to the very edge of the show-ring, just as the judge called for the last class of the day: "Teams for general use!" Eliza held her breath. The crowd at the far

side of the ring moved back and Father proudly drove Champ and Monarch into the ring. Trotting behind came a team of bays. Last in were an older team of white horses. The three farmers drove their teams around the ring for the judge.

A gentleman newly arrived in Canada boasted, "Those workhorses are not nearly as big as the ones back home. Our English workhorse has enormous strength."

Eliza felt like stamping on his foot. The upstart was put

in his place by a burly farmer. "Yes, and get stuck behind them on the road, and you'll not be home till next week! Our Canadian horse can do the heavy field work and is also a good road horse. So, ya see, we've got an animal nobly suited for both jobs."

The judge called for the drivers to reverse. The bays, jittery from the noise of the spectators, hesitated before obeying the rein. Father reined his team in the opposite direction by doing a figure eight. The steady jingle of the harness told Eliza that Champ and Monarch had not missed a step.

"Perfect!" whispered Eliza.

"That's 'cause Papa's a fine horseman. Everyone knows that," added James.

The teams drew up in a steady line and the judge inspected each one.

"In first place," the judge called out, "is the team of blacks, owned by Mr. William Newberry. They show finely formed limbs, great shoulder power, and are an all-around capital pair of horses."

As Father was handed the first-place ticket, he proudly tipped his hat to the judge and spectators.

Eliza, Thomas and James whooped with joy until a stern look from Mother told Eliza that she must contain herself.

Bubbling with happiness, Eliza asked, "May we have our candy treat now, please, Mamma?"

"Certainly, Eliza. You may go with James to make your purchase while Father ties up the team." Mother returned the two halfpennies to Eliza.

At the Yankee pedlar's wagon, Eliza handed over her money as the pedlar rolled a brown paper into a cone, filled it with horehound candy and twisted the ends shut. She gave James his treat, took one out for herself, and tucked the rest into her pocket to share with Thomas later. James' candy was soon gone and he happily licked his lips, but Eliza had not waited all day to have her special treat disappear. Slowly she savoured the tangy sweetness.

Nearby, the musical entertainment was beginning on a platform gaily skirted with a banner of patriotic colours. People were drawn to the music and soon the Newberrys were encircled by the crowd. Fiddle, fife and drum accom-

panied the Hillmore Boys' Choir as they sang "The Gambler's Wife", "Fancy's Dream", "Woodman Spare that Tree" and other favourite songs. Then, the musicians struck up a lively tune. To Eliza's surprise Mr. Donovan, a big barrel of a man, began jigging about. Soon other saucy men joined him, and a great number of people were roughly jostled. Suddenly, Mr. Donovan stumbled into Eliza. He reeked of a strange, sweet odour. Even Mother was alarmed.

Just then Eliza saw Father. He was slowly working his way towards them chatting with the men he met. Father's friendly banter made the crowd seem less frightening. Once Father was beside them, Eliza felt safe.

"William," said Mother indignantly. "Such a pleasant affair is spoilt by the intemperance of so many men!"

Father smiled reassuringly. "It is unfortunate Mary, but it has been a grand day for the Newberrys."

Just then Mr. Charles Edwards, the Agricultural Society's president, stepped up onto the platform. To conclude the day he spoke about the accomplishments of the Society and a plan to increase admission fees to allow the Society to build a proper Exhibition Hall. Father and the other folks that agreed encouraged him with cheers and clapping. Others booed and yelled. All in all, Eliza thought, it was a very long and tiresome speech.

By the time Mr. Edwards had finished, the afternoon sun was casting long black shadows over the grounds. It was time to collect their prize money, gather up their entries and start for home.

Thomas yawned. "Papa sure won lots and lots of money."

"Yes, lad," replied Father, "a man would have to do a good week's work to earn the six dollars and fifty cents we've won today." Then Father smiled and picked Thomas up in his arms. "I guess the Newberry family will be getting that coal-oil lamp."

Eliza gave Father a big hug. He answered with a wink. Eliza could only grin at her thoughts: Papa's buying my coal-oil lamp. I've won my first premium, kept secret James' visit to Professor Grant, and had the most delicious treat. Today is the best Wednesday in my whole life!

Historical Note

Eliza's Best Wednesday is set in Canada West. Canada West had been called Upper Canada until 1841, when Upper Canada (now Ontario) and Lower Canada (now Quebec) were joined into one colony, the Province of Canada. No one could agree on where the capital of the colony should be, so there was a compromise: from 1851-1865 the capital moved from Quebec City to Toronto every four years. The capital was in Quebec City in 1860, the year in which *Eliza's Best Wednesday* takes place.

The government was much smaller than it is today, but moving every four years was very inefficient, so Queen Victoria decided that a permanent capital would be built in Ottawa. Work on the Parliament Buildings began in 1859.

During the summer of 1860, the Prince of Wales toured the British North American colonies. No member of the British royal family had ever visited before. Large crowds flocked to see the Prince and much celebration accompanied the event. But perhaps the most exciting part of his visit was laying the cornerstone for the new Parliament Buildings.

Eliza's family would have read about these events in their local newspaper, but to farming families like Eliza's, the agricultural exhibition was likely the most important event of the season.

The population of Canada West was approximately 1,300,000 people. Toronto was the largest city, with more than 40,000 residents; however, most families (such as

Eliza's) lived on farms. Farming occupied most of the population in Canada West. Farm families raised pigs, cattle and sheep for meat. They kept cows for milk, butter and cheese, and chickens for meat and eggs. They also grew wheat and hay, vegetables and fruit. In fact, they grew almost all of their food. What they couldn't grow — salt, sugar and spices — they bought from the general store.

Where did they get money from? They might sell wheat to the local mill owner, who would grind the wheat into flour and sell it. The farmers might also take some of their farm produce to the general store to settle their debt and purchase items such as sugar, salt, kerosene, spices, cotton, dishes and hardware. The merchants would then sell the farmers' fruit, eggs, butter and vegetables to local townspeople.

Farmers sometimes made extra money by using their horses and wagons to help people move house or transport heavy loads. They might also sell products made from trees from their land: firewood, barrel staves and fence rails.

The merchants, mill owners and tradesmen earned their living by selling wares to the farmers; so everyone, in the towns and on the farms, hoped for a good harvest each year. In order that the farmers could learn about new ways to increase their harvests and make their work easier, people formed agricultural societies. These groups held regular meetings to share their knowledge and experience. Members would talk about all sorts of things to do with running a farm, such as whether a new type of farm machinery was worth buying, or types of fruit and vegetables that grew well in cold weather.

In order to encourage the farmers to do their best, agricultural societies held exhibitions. Prize money — as much as a man would earn in a day — was given to the members entering the best examples of various types of livestock, crops, fruit and vegetables. There were also prizes for home-made items such as weaving, bread, maple sugar, honey and quilting.

In 1860, only men could belong to the agricultural societies, even though their wives and daughters worked just as hard as they did. Often, all entries would have the father's name on them, even such things as needlework or weaving, which were done by the female members of the family.

To encourage farmers to buy labour-saving machinery, manufacturers of stoves and gadgets and farm equipment also came to the exhibitions. Where else could they get the whole community together to show them their latest inventions and newest models? This part of the exhibitions was much like modern shows that display such things as tools or appliances or farm machinery.

The exhibitions came in the fall, right after the hard work of harvesting, when farmers saw the results of their whole year's work. People looked forward to seeing their friends and neighbours at the exhibition. For in those days keeping in touch wasn't just a matter of picking up the telephone. (People could keep in touch by letter, but postage was quite expensive.)

The people and town in *Eliza's Best Wednesday* are made up, but they are based on facts we know about Canada West in 1860. We looked at newspapers, pictures, letters and items in museums from the time. From these we could accurately recreate a typical exhibition. All the details in the text and pictures are based on this research. We made the Newberry family and their farm quite successful: they have good land and are skilled farmers. As would be expected in 1860, Mr. Newberry makes all the decisions for the family and the farm.

In the 1860s, boys and girls were treated very differently. James could be adventurous and get away with being disobedient in small things; but Eliza would be expected to be ladylike: she must watch her manners and not shout or be rowdy. If Eliza were a ten-year-old today, many of her skills would still be put to use on a modern farm; but she might be able to have more noisy fun.

Glossary

Artful swindler: a cunning cheat.

Calico: a printed cotton fabric.

Candlesconce: a metal candleholder.

Coop: a cage or pen for poultry.

Copper: a penny.

Cravat: a band with an attached bow worn over the shirt collar.

Crock: an earthenware pot or jar.

Democrat: a square-box wagon with two to four moveable seats used for work on the farm as well as for pleasure.

Firkin: a small wooden barrel.

Flannel: a soft woven woollen fabric.

Frockcoat: a man's knee-length suit coat.

Halfpenny: a copper coin valued at one-half of a penny.

Harrow: a farm instrument used to break up and even off ploughed ground.

Horehound: a bitter-sweet mint.

Intemperance: the excessive drinking of alcohol.

Mutton: the meat from a sheep.

Nine-patch: a quilt pattern with each block consisting of nine squares.

Patriotic colours: red, white and blue, the colours of the Union Jack.

Phrenologist: a person who can tell people's character and intelligence by the outer appearance and shape of their skull.

Quack doctor: a person who pretends a knowledge of medical skills.

Quill pen: a pen made from a feather which is dipped in ink for writing.

Roan: a reddish brown animal coat mixed with white hair.

Settee: a long seat with a back, for use indoors.

Spinster: an unmarried woman.

Union Jack: the national flag of the United Kingdom. In 1860 it was the flag of the British Empire including Canada West.

Waistcoat: a man's vest.

Yankee pedlar: a travelling American pedlar.